The Giving Bear

Disney's
Winnie the Pooh First Readers

A Winnie the Pooh First Reader

The Giving Bear

Isabel Gaines

ILLUSTRATED BY Josie Yee

DISNEY
PRESS

NEW YORK

The Giving Bear

"Umph!" grunted Piglet

as he knocked on Pooh's door.

He had his wagon with him.

It was loaded with stuff.

"Hello, Piglet," answered Pooh.

"What's in your wagon?"

"Things from my house,"
Piglet said. "I'm giving them
to Christopher Robin."

Just then Tigger bounced up.

"Hello!" he said.

He had his wagon, too.

"Hello, Tigger," said Pooh.

"Are you giving your things

to Christopher Robin, too?"

"Yes," answered Tigger.

"So he can give them

to someone who needs them."

"Do you have anything
you don't need anymore,
Pooh?" asked Piglet.

"Let me think," said Pooh,

thinking very hard.

But he couldn't think

of a thing.

13

Along came Christopher Robin.

"I see Piglet's and Tigger's wagons,"

he said. "Are you going

to add anything, Pooh?"

15

"I don't have anything
to give away,"
Pooh said sadly.
"There must be something,"
said Tigger.

"Let's look in the cupboard,"

suggested Piglet.

Pooh opened the cupboard doors.

17

"Oh, dear!" said Piglet.

"Zowee!" shouted Tigger.

"Wow!" exclaimed Christopher Robin.

"Twenty honeypots!" they said

at the same time.

"Only ten honeypots

have any honey

in them," Christopher Robin said.

"I keep a large supply
of honeypots at all times,"
said Pooh.

"Why is that, Pooh Bear?"
asked Christopher Robin.

"Just in case," announced Pooh.

"In case of what?" asked Piglet.

He was a little afraid

to hear the answer.

"I might find

some especially

yummy honey," Pooh said.

"I would need plenty of pots

to store it in,

so I would never run out."

"ALL honey tastes
especially yummy to you!"
Christopher Robin
reminded Pooh gently.

"Ten pots are more than enough

to store your yummy honey."

"But what if I had a party?"

asked Pooh.

"Everyone would want

some honey,

so I would need a lot."

"Pooh," Christopher Robin said,

"if you had a party,

you would invite your friends

in the Hundred-Acre Wood."

"Ten honeypots hold
more than enough honey
for us," said Piglet.

"Hmm," said Pooh.

He still wasn't sure

he wanted to give away

his honeypots.

"Think of everyone
who could enjoy some honey
if you shared your honeypots,"
said Christopher Robin.

"Then they would all be
as happy as I am!" agreed Pooh.

Pooh decided to give away
ten of his honeypots.

His heart felt twice its size.

"Silly old bear," said

Christopher Robin.

He helped Pooh load

his honeypots onto his wagon.